Mrs. Meredith Grace
and the
Secret of Books

Tales for the Imaginative Mind

WRITTEN AND ILLUSTRATED BY
SAMANTHA CALLEN

For my daughters, Lillian and Alexandria.

Thank you for inspiring me.
I hope you continue to always feed your
imagination by reading!

Library of Congress Control Number 2022917352
Published in the United States by Wild Child Education Co.
ISBN 978-1-7342645-4-8

For more information, or to book an event, visit our website:
www.wildchildeducationco.com

This book belongs to:

_____

_____

You Are About

Who Can Travel Any

To Meet A Person

where Using A Book!

Meet
Mrs. Meredith Grace

A connoisseur of books galore!
She loves to discover
and knows there is more
to the story,
just past the cover!

A **connoisseur** you say?
Why yes, it's true!

She'll tell you herself...

"I read and read those
books on the shelves!"

You see, Mrs. Meredith Grace is a librarian by day.

But at night,
she can use her books
to travel far, far away.

She knows the secret.
Oh yes, she does...

And if you listen quite closely
and promise to keep it, she just
might share it with you.

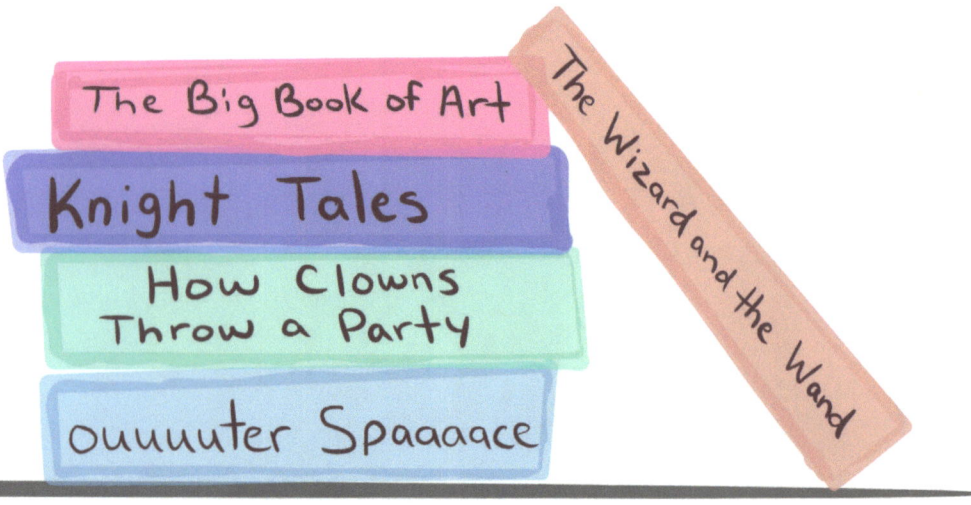

Do you want to **learn** the secret of all these wonderful books?

You can travel **at will** when you **open** a book!

Mrs. Grace can not wait to get into her nook!

After the children all leave...

It's off she goes!
Being careful to watch her head,
fingers and toes.

Oh, goodness! Watch out!
It's a PIE THROWING contest
with clowns all about!

All clear here!

Whew, that was close! No pie in the face?

You've got **quick** moves!

Want to try another book?
Come on, let's go!

A book about **Knights** and
a **blacksmith**.

What is that?
We are going to find out!
Let's go, quick!

Knight Tales

Into the next book…
Oh, wow look at that!
It is a **horse** and a **knight**.
There is also a **blacksmith**,
making things just right.

Whoa! That was neat!
Did you see the anvil?
Blacksmiths use tools to work
with metals.

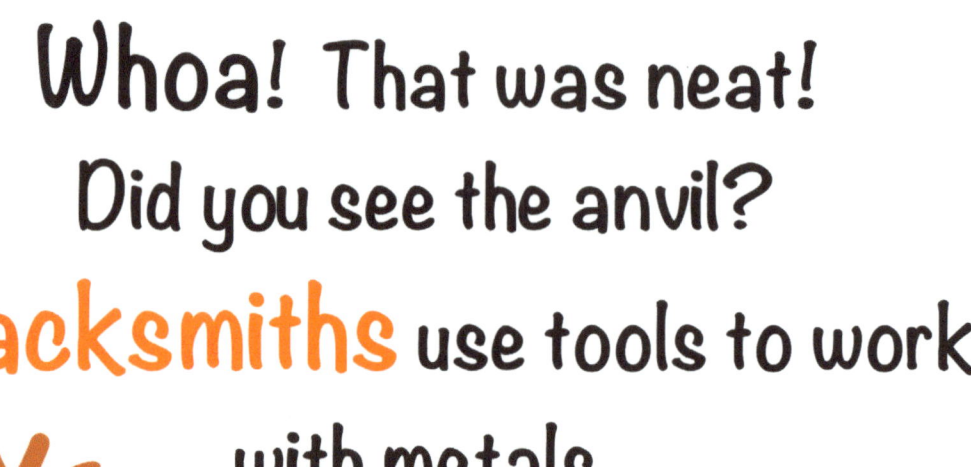

Bending
and **melting**
the metals
together.

I'm ready for another book.
Are you ready, too?

A book about **underwater**

adventures.

Are you ready to explore?

How to Live Underwater for
Beginners

Do you see what I see?
Yes, that's a shark!
You'd better hunch down.

They are big, but not mean.
They just want to swim around.
I think we'll move on though,
he might be **hungry**!

I'm no fish and neither are you.
Quick, let's hurry!

Did you see that **hammerhead shark**?

How about the fish, the turtle and coral?

It is pretty neat visiting **the Great Barrier Reef**.

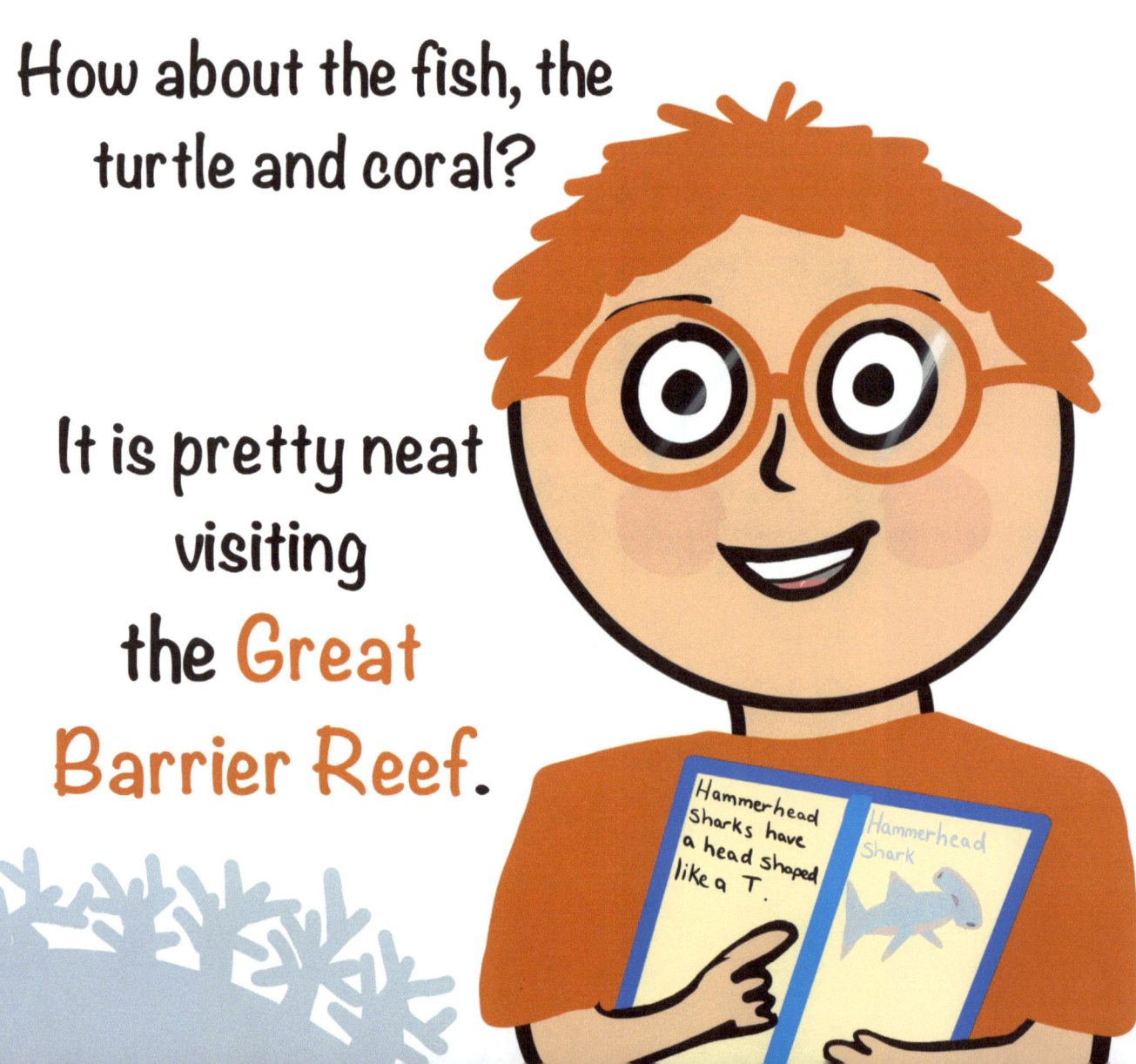

Hammerhead Sharks have a head shaped like a T.

Hammerhead Shark

All of these travels are making

me hungry.

Let's look for a bite of our own!

Into the next book,

here we go!

Foods of the World

Oh, my. Look at that!
It's the Eiffel Tower in France.
Great place for a snack!

They have **croissants** and **baguettes**.

They taste so good with a bit of butter on top.

Mmmmm...That was good! Are you full now?

Are you ready for the next adventure?

Time to **jump** into the next book!

It's a book of art!
This looks cool!

What do you think we'll find?

Ready?
Let's go!

Oh, my! This is a little different.
IT'S OKAY, IT'S JUST ART!

Shapes or zigzags, even splashes of color...

No two pieces are alike, even if
made like the other.
Can you spot the differences
in the pictures above?

Okay, now on to the next book!

A book about magic, a wizard and spells. We will have to be careful, we will have to watch out!

Potions and spells on the table.
A book to turn people to owls!
I don't want to fly today, thanks.

Whew! That was close!

Anyone with feathers?
No? Okay, good!
Told you reading was an
adventure!
Ready for the next book?

I'm getting a little sleepy,
how about a camp out under
the Northern Lights?

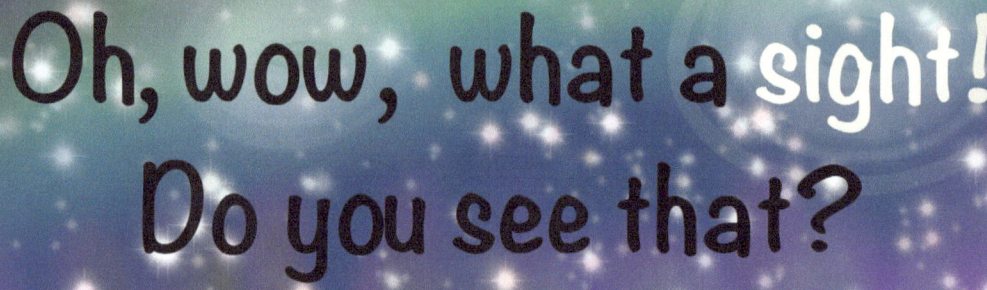

Oh, wow, what a sight!
Do you see that?

The Aurora Borealis,
so beautiful and bright.
All of those colors light up
the night.

Oh, wow! That was so **wild** to see!
Those lights were dazzling,
wouldn't you agree?

The **Aurora Borealis** happens with help from the sun.

Okay, one more **adventure** before we are done!

It's ouuuuuter spaaaaace!

Can you see the planets
Mercury, Venus, Earth and Mars?

The moon is
there too,
it's never too far.

Our sun also helps to create the
Aurora Borealis that we saw.
Did you know that people
go to space?

Oh, wow, wow, wow!!!

That was so amazing. So far out!

What does it make you think about?

There are 8 planets in total!
Do you know them all?

Mercury, Venus,
Earth, Mars, Jupiter,
Saturn, Uranus, and
Neptune!

Ouuuter Spaaaace!

People really do go to space you know!
They launch into space on rockets.
You also need more than just a
helmet because there is

no air in space to breathe!

We used to only have astronauts in space, but
one day, it could be
you or me!
A man named Elon Musk builds
rockets to help.
We all live on Earth but, people want to
travel to Mars!

Did you have fun? I hope you did!
You can learn anything
and travel anywhere when you
open a book!

What will you learn and where will you go next?

There are so **many** books to read!
And maybe one day,
You'll go on an adventure just like this!

www.ingramcontent.com/pod-product-compliance
Lightning Source LLC
Chambersburg PA
CBHW041011170626
46815CB00003B/261